One Baby Jesus

Un Niño Dios

One Baby Jesus

Un Niño Dios

by Patricia A. Pingry
Translated by Aide Urbano

Illustrated by
Wendy Edelson

ideals children's books™
Nashville, Tennessee

ISBN 0-8249-5472-6

Published by Ideals Children's Books
An imprint of Ideals Publications
A division of Guideposts
535 Metroplex Drive, Suite 250
Nashville, Tennessee 37211
www.idealsbooks.com

Color separations by Precision Color Graphics
Franklin, Wisconsin

Printed and bound in Mexico by RR Donnelley

Library of Congress CIP data on file

Cover design by Marisa Calvin
Book design by Jenny Eber Hancock

3 5 7 9 10 8 6 4 2

To Parents and Teachers:

One Baby Jesus, Un Niño Dios, is one of a series of bilingual books specially created by Ideals Children's Books to help children and their parents learn to read both Spanish and English.

Whether the child's native language is English or Spanish, he or she will be able to compare the text and, thus, learn to read both English and Spanish.

Also included at the end of the story are several common words listed in both English and Spanish that the child may review. These include both nouns, with their gender in Spanish, and verbs. In the case of the verbs, the Spanish verbs have the endings that indicate their use in the story.

Parents and teachers will want to use this book as a beginning reader for children who speak either English or Spanish.

A los Padres y los Maestros:

One Baby Jesus, Un Niño Dios, es parte de una serie de libros bilingüe hecho especialmente por Ideals Children's Books para ayudar a los niños y a sus padres a aprender como leer en Español e Inglés.

Cualquiera que sea el idioma nativo, el Inglés o el Español, el niño podrá comparar lo escrito y entonces aprenderá como leer en Inglés y en Español.

Al final de la historia hay una lista de vocabulario con palabras comunes en Inglés y en Español. La lista tiene ambos sustantivos, con el género y verbos en Español con los fines que indican el uso en la historia.

Los padres y los maestros desearán usar este libro como nivel inicial de lectura para niños que hablan Inglés o Español.

On the first day of Christmas, my mama gave to me
one baby Jesus sleeping peacefully.

En el primer día de Navidad, mi mamá me dio
un niño Dios durmiendo tranquilamente.

On the second day of Christmas, my mama gave to me
two parents smiling,
and one baby Jesus sleeping peacefully.

En el segundo día de Navidad, mi mamá me dio
dos padres sonriendo,
y un niño Dios durmiendo tranquilamente.

On the third day of Christmas, my mama gave to me
three wise men giving, two parents smiling,
and one baby Jesus sleeping peacefully.

En el tercer día de Navidad, mi mamá me dio
tres reyes magos con regalos, dos padres sonriendo,
y un niño Dios durmiendo tranquilamente.

On the fourth day of Christmas, my mama gave to me
four camels plodding, three wise men giving,
two parents smiling,
and one baby Jesus sleeping peacefully.

En el cuarto día de Navidad, mi mamá me dio
cuatro camellos cansados, tres reyes magos con regalos,
dos padres sonriendo,
y un niño Dios durmiendo tranquilamente.

On the fifth day of Christmas, my mama gave to me
five golden stars, four camels plodding,
three wise men giving, two parents smiling,
and one baby Jesus sleeping peacefully.

En el quinto día de Navidad, mi mamá me dio
cinco estrellas doradas, cuatro camellos cansados,
tres reyes magos con regalos, dos padres sonriendo,
y un niño Dios durmiendo tranquilamente.

On the sixth day of Christmas, my mama gave to me
six donkeys braying, five golden stars,
four camels plodding,
three wise men giving, two parents smiling,
and one baby Jesus sleeping peacefully.

En el sexto día de Navidad, mi mamá me dio
seis burros rebuznando, cinco estrellas doradas,
cuatro camellos cansados,
tres reyes magos con regalos, dos padres sonriendo,
y un niño Dios durmiendo tranquilamente.

On the seventh day of Christmas, my mama gave to me
seven shepherds kneeling, six donkeys braying,
five golden stars, four camels plodding,
three wise men giving, two parents smiling,
and one baby Jesus sleeping peacefully.

En el séptimo día de Navidad, mi mamá me dio
siete pastores arrodillados, seis burros rebuznando,
cinco estrellas doradas, cuatro camellos cansados,
tres reyes magos con regalos, dos padres sonriendo,
y un niño Dios durmiendo tranquilamente.

On the eighth day of Christmas, my mama gave to me
eight angels singing, seven shepherds kneeling,
six donkeys braying, five golden stars,
four camels plodding, three wise men giving,
two parents smiling,
and one baby Jesus sleeping peacefully.

En el octavo día de Navidad, mi mamá me dio
ocho ángeles cantando, siete pastores arrodillados,
seis burros rebuznando, cinco estrellas doradas,
cuatro camellos cansados, tres reyes magos con regalos,
dos padres sonriendo,
y un niño Dios durmiendo tranquilamente.

On the ninth day of Christmas, my mama gave to me
nine lambs cavorting, eight angels singing,
seven shepherds kneeling, six donkeys braying,
five golden stars, four camels plodding,
three wise men giving, two parents smiling,
and one baby Jesus sleeping peacefully.

En el noveno día de Navidad, mi mamá me dio
nueve borregos jugando, ocho ángeles cantando,
siete pastores arrodillados, seis burros rebuznando,
cinco estrellas doradas, cuatro camellos cansados,
tres reyes magos con regalos, dos padres sonriendo,
y un niño Dios durmiendo tranquilamente.

On the tenth day of Christmas, my mama gave to me
ten cows a-mooing, nine lambs cavorting,
eight angels singing, seven shepherds kneeling,
six donkeys braying, five golden stars,
four camels plodding,
three wise men giving, two parents smiling,
and one baby Jesus sleeping peacefully.

En el décimo día de Navidad, mi mamá me dio
diez vacas mugiendo, nueve borregos jugando,
ocho ángeles cantando, siete pastores arrodillados,
seis burros rebuznando, cinco estrellas doradas,
cuatro camellos cansados,
tres reyes magos con regalos, dos padres sonriendo,
y un niño Dios durmiendo tranquilamente.

On the eleventh day of Christmas, my mama gave to me
eleven doves a-cooing, ten cows a-mooing,
nine lambs cavorting, eight angels singing,
seven shepherds kneeling, six donkeys braying,
five golden stars, four camels plodding,
three wise men giving, two parents smiling,
and one baby Jesus sleeping peacefully.

En el undécimo día de Navidad, mi mamá me dio
once palomas arrullando, diez vacas mugiendo,
nueve borregos jugando, ocho ángeles cantando,
siete pastores arrodillados, seis burros rebuznando,
cinco estrellas doradas, cuatro camellos cansados,
tres reyes magos con regalos, dos padres sonriendo,
y un niño Dios durmiendo tranquilamente.

On the twelfth day of Christmas, my mama gave to me
twelve hugs and kisses, eleven doves a-cooing,
ten cows a-mooing, nine lambs cavorting,
eight angels singing, seven shepherds kneeling,
six donkeys braying, five golden stars,
four camels plodding, three wise men giving,
two parents smiling,
and one baby Jesus sleeping peacefully.

En el duodécimo día de Navidad, mi mamá me dio
doce besos y abrazos, once palomas arrullando,
diez vacas mugiendo, nueve borregos jugando,
ocho ángeles cantando, siete pastores arrodillados,
seis burros rebuznando, cinco estrellas doradas,
cuatro camellos cansados, tres reyes magos con regalos,
dos padres sonriendo,
y un niño Dios durmiendo tranquilamente.

Vocabulary words used in
One Baby Jesus
Un Niño Dios

English	Spanish	English	Spanish
Christmas	de Navidad	smiling	sonriendo
day	el día	third	tercer
first	primer	three	tres
mama	mamá	wise men	reyes magos
sleeping	durmiendo	fourth	cuarto
peacefully	tranquilamente	four	cuatro
baby Jesus	niño Dios	camels	camellos
on	en	plodding	cansados
second	segundo	fifth	quinto
two	dos	five	cinco
parents	padres	golden	doradas

English	Spanish	English	Spanish
stars	estrellas	nine	nueve
sixth	sexto	lambs	borregos
six	seis	cavorting	jugando
donkeys	burros	eleventh	undécimo
braying	rebuznando	eleven	once
seventh	séptimo	doves	palomas
seven	siete	a-cooing	arrullando
shepherds	pastores	twelfth	duodécimo
kneeling	arrodillados	twelve	doce
eighth	octavo	hugs	abrazos
eight	ocho	and	y
angels	ángeles	kisses	besos
singing	cantando		
ninth	noveno